THE WEDDING CAKE MURDER

BAKERS AND BULLDOG MYSTERIES BOOK 12

ROSIE SAMS

SWEETBOOKHUB.COM

Rosie is a member of SweetBookHub, a place where you can find
amazing fun books that are all sweet and suitable for all ages. Join
the exclusive newsletter and get 3 free books here

"*T*his place is positively beautiful!" gasped Melody Marshall to Kerry Porter, her dear friend and business partner in their pastry shop, *Decadently Delicious*. The two were visiting the newly renovated Bronwyn's Country Inn, where Kerry would soon marry her fiancé, Bradford Smedley.

Melody was slightly surprised that Kerry wanted to come back; their last visit to the place had ended in murder. But Kerry had fallen in love with the inn, and this was her opportunity to check over the final details before her big day.

As she spun slowly on the spot, Melody's eyes widened. The panoramic view of the inn's newly restored English gardens was simply breathtaking. They had entered the garden through the French doors of the main dining room. Those doors led to an outdoor patio made of large flat brown and gray stones with a smattering of outdoor café style tables. Two symmetrical ivy topiaries carefully manicured in spiral shapes decorated with white pin lights marked the entrance to the gardens. The walkway was covered in white and gray gravel. The small pebbles glittered like diamonds when the sun hit them just right. The pathway was also lined with short symmetrical hedges that squared off four open lawn spaces of beautiful green.

Each garden was separated by another path, just like the one leading away from the inn. From a bird's eye view, these paths made a perfect cross between the gardens, and it was stunning.

Guests were welcome to play some of the outdoor games Bronwyn had set up on the lawns such as croquet or horseshoes. In the very center of each path, raised flower beds of marigolds, hydrangea, and hibiscus, to name a few, brought color and butterflies to the gardens. Green shrubs helped disguise beautifully decorated birdbaths, hand-painted birdhouses, and hidden stone benches that were strategically placed along the way. It was at the very center of the paths, where they all joined, that Melody and Kerry now stood. Together, they surveyed the grounds under a beautiful white trellis decorated with sheer white curtains that blew in the soft breeze. That same breeze carried the sweet scent of the garden's blooming red, pink, and yellow roses along with the delicate white rambling roses that climbed the bridal trellis.

"This is the exact spot!" Kerry said as she planted her feet, marking where she would pledge her eternal love to Bradford.

Melody quickly stepped whimsically into the groom's spot.

"I do, take thee, Kerry, in baking and business, 'til death do us part," Melody joked as she mimicked Bradford's deep masculine voice.

"I do, take thee, Melody, in frosting and fondant, 'til death do us part," laughed Kerry as she pressed her hands to her heart, overdramatizing the moment. Together, they shared a laugh that ended in deep sighs for them both as they anticipated tomorrow's big event.

Deeper in the gardens, Smudge, Melody's lovable blue-gray French Bulldog, explored, twitching her little wet nose at the various flowers and bugs she discovered. When she trotted back to where the friends were standing, she had a stray daisy caught in her collar.

"And right on cue, here comes the flower girl." Melody smiled at Smudge. She bent down and scratched her adorable pup's ears.

Even as a young girl, Kerry knew the inn was the perfect venue for her dream wedding. In fact, after Bradford proposed, the first phone call she'd made was not to her mother, father, or sister, but to the then proprietor of the inn. A lot had happened since then, and it was now Coleman Urquhart who had bought the quaint but faltering inn and restored its original elegance, making Bronwyn's the most sought-after wedding venue for miles around Port Warren. Kerry hadn't hesitated to lock in her date.

The inn was a renovated English style stone mansion originally constructed in the 1800s. Visitors traveled a private graveled driveway that branched off one of Port Warren's main roadways to get there. The driveway ended in a circular loop around a restored water fountain. The mansion was just on the other side of the loop, opposite the fountain. Its exterior brown-gray stone walls were covered in lush green ivy. It had a wide-open lobby with a staircase leading up to its twenty guest rooms, two parlors, and one main dining hall that was surrounded by French doors that led to a maze of English gardens. The wedding ceremony would be held in the gardens, followed by a celebration back in the main dining hall, complete with a wooden dance floor and crystal chandeliers. The new Bronwyn's Country Inn was nothing short of spectacular.

"Isn't it just like a fairy tale, Mel?" Kerry asked while she conducted her final walkthrough of the garden's restored elegance. "I'm so ready for my happy ending!"

"Everything will be perfect, Kerry. I'm sure of it."

"Hey!" A familiar voice called toward Melody and Kerry. It was Leslie Mathers, the close friend and business partner of both Melody and Kerry. They made a fine trio.

"The kitchen staff are ready for us to bring in the cake!" Leslie yelled across the garden as she stood waving from an open set of French doors. Smudge barked happily as she appeared from the gardens and bounded toward Leslie.

"I planned every detail exactly like I've always dreamed and in such a way that nothing should go wrong... *except for one thing*," Kelly said. Her voice transitioned from excited to worried in the matter of a single sentence.

"What are you worried about? The staff here is top-notch. The view is stunning, and the best pastry chef in the country handcrafted your customized wedding cake." Melody flashed Kerry a playful grin, as she had made the wedding cake.

Kerry's steps halted abruptly just as she was about to cross the threshold from the garden into the main dining hall.

"It's my sister, Kim," Kerry answered both Melody's question and announced her sister's arrival. Her expression was grave.

Inside, a woman who could easily pass for Kerry chatted politely with Leslie. As Kerry stepped into the doorway, Leslie looked relieved to see her. "Oh, look, Kim," Leslie interrupted Kim's tale of travel woes. "Here, she is!" Leslie's voice sounded a bit too enthusiastic.

Kerry and her sister, Kim Porter Anders, had been estranged for some time now. Their relationship was strained due to Kim's husband, Jared Anders. Melody and Leslie found it hard to make conversation with Kim on the odd occasion she called the bakery looking for Kerry. Usually, those phone calls left Kerry sad and distracted for the entire day. It was obvious to Melody that Leslie was waiting for an excuse to exit the conversation.

"Hi, Kim. It's good to see you. Leslie, let's go get the cake into the walk-in," Melody said as she picked up on Leslie's need to escape. Smudge trotted alongside Melody, eager to assist.

"Hello, Melody... and Smudge!" Kim said. Then, she threw her arms up in the air and ran toward her sister, fully intending to hug her. "Kerry! You've outdone yourself! This place is like a *little* storybook cottage! Sure, it's not as big as where Jared and I got married, but still, it's great. My only wish is that your day is as special as ours was and that you and Bradford are as happy as Jared and I."

Kerry extended her arms toward her sister inviting her in for a hug. At first, she smiled, but once her chin rested firmly on Kim's shoulder, Kerry's expression changed to one of sadness. Deep in her heart, she knew her sister didn't intend to insult her venue, but she also knew that her sister was struggling with her own marriage. Jared wasn't as nice as he could be to Kim and Kerry often worried about her sister's happiness. As a result, Kerry found herself keeping her distance from her sister, and that separation hurt most. As Kerry pulled back from the hug, she took Kim's hands in hers. "It's perfect for Bradford and me. How was your trip into Port Warren?" Kerry asked. While Kerry waited for Kim's answer, she realized how tired Kim looked. Her eyes were puffy and watery as if she had been crying.

"It was..." Kim's voice trailed off as Jared entered the main dining hall. The very sound of his footsteps caused her to squeeze her eyes shut and her body to stiffen. Kerry noticed the change in Kim's body language right away. He was distracted by his cellphone, texting as he walked. He didn't bother to look up and greet anyone.

"Of course, the room isn't ready. I guess you get what

you pay for," Jared huffed, his words insinuating the venue choice was second rate.

Jared Anders was a hot-shot businessman. He married Kim Porter just after college graduation. They were high school sweethearts with a typical teen love story. He was the captain of the football team. She was the captain of the cheerleading team. He proposed at the Homecoming dance. She accepted immediately. Surprisingly, their romance lasted through college, even though they attended different schools. Kim found out about several of Jared's indiscretions, but she forgave them, writing them off as college exploration. Perhaps, he just needed to get it out of his system.

But as Jared gained more confidence and became successful in his business career, the more poorly he treated Kim. To Kerry's knowledge, he didn't physically abuse her, but his sense of entitlement grew, and he treated Kim like she was his servant rather than his partner. Kerry was unable to convince Kim that the marriage wasn't a good one, and as a result, their relationship was strained.

With glassy eyes, Kim pulled away from Kerry and

headed toward Jared. "I'll go talk with the front desk. I'm sure it's just a misunderstanding."

Kerry inhaled sharply as she watched her sister try to accommodate the selfish little man that thought himself a king. Quietly, she said to herself, "Yep... as happy as you two are."

CHAPTER TWO

*M*elody and Leslie removed the Porter-Smedley wedding cake and a large sheet cake for the rehearsal dinner from the back of their new Decadently Delicious delivery van while Smudge waited at the curbside. The van was about the size of a standard SUV. Instead of a backseat and trunk area, the entire back was remodeled as a large rectangular shaped refrigerator compartment. It was big enough for multiple tier wedding cakes, such as Kerry's. There were two side access doors where an SUV would normally have passenger doors. There were also two back doors that opened wide, much like a standard van. There was even a little lift function making it easier to slide cakes out and lower them to a rolling cart. The rolling cart was perfect for safely delivering the cakes to their final venue.

With the new refrigerated delivery van, Decadently Delicious was able to expand its service area to neighboring towns. Plus, with the outside of the van wrapped to advertise the bakery, the mobile billboard was an investment worth every penny.

Together, they carefully pushed the rolling cart carrying Kerry's dream cake toward the kitchen of Bronwyn's. Smudge trotted along behind them, her ears up and alert. There, Coleman reviewed the details of the dinner service with his executive chef, his full-time staff, and the additional wait staff hired to accommodate a wedding of this unusual size. Bronwyn's weddings were typically a more intimate size. It was clear that Coleman was stressed. By his tone and body language, Melody sensed he didn't have much faith in his staff either.

As the Decadently Delicious rolling cart entered the kitchen, Coleman stopped speaking. His eyes took in the beautiful wedding cake. The cake was five tiers high. Instead of the tiers gradually getting smaller as they were stacked higher, these tiers were all the same size giving the cake a more modern, elegant appearance. Each tier was covered in eggshell-colored fondant. Flecks of gold smattered the fondant giving it a glittered effect. Horizontally and vertically centered, six red rosebuds adorned each tier. Atop the cake sat two white porcelain love birds. It was Kerry's mother's wedding cake topper.

"Melody, that cake is just divine! What flavor is it?" Coleman asked curiously. Behind him, the chef and staff applauded the cake.

Smudge sat up straight and proud as if she had made the cake herself.

"The yellow cake has a light lemon flavor. It's coated in a white chocolate buttercream underneath the fondant." Melody blushed at the applause and playfully offered a curtsy in return. "The sheet cake is a strawberry shortcake for the rehearsal dinner."

"Here, let me help you with that," the chef said as he approached the rolling cart. He took over for Melody and helped Leslie guide the cakes into the walk-in refrigerator.

"I'm sure the guests will go crazy over both," Coleman said. He turned back toward the staff to finish preparations and noticed one of the additional hires was on her cell phone... again. She had been texting through the whole final walkthrough, and Coleman didn't appreciate it one bit.

Bronwyn's Country Inn was a Port Warren landmark, but it was no secret that the inn had experienced its share of troubles in the past. With Coleman's recent takeover, his first order of business was to fire the majority of the staff. His problem, however, was finding suitable replacements.

"Liza, I've told you repeatedly, put your phone away. Weddings are serious business, and I won't have you ruining some bride's most special occasion," Coleman warned impatiently. "When you're here, and I'm paying you, your attention should be on nothing else but Bronwyn's."

Liza Summers slipped behind another new hire to hide her rolling her ocean blue eyes. She tucked her cell phone into the back pocket of her black work pants and huffed. She was an attractive young woman with impeccable bone structure and long blond hair swept up into a messy bun that Coleman would address after the preparation session. Coleman presumed she was probably an aspiring actress or model waitressing to make ends meet until she hit it big. He noticed she had a chip on her shoulder. He wasn't exactly a poor judge of character and had spotted that Liza really disliked working at the inn. She had very little interest in watching couples wed or any other formal event for that matter. Liza had one goal in mind when working this kind of gig – *find a wealthy, unhappily married, older gentleman that she could con into paying her way.* Her boss, however, was repeatedly getting in her way. At the last wedding event she worked for at Bronwyn's, she had met a wonderful candidate. The man was in his late fifties. He was a widower of three years and not quite yet confident enough to start dating again, but then he saw Liza. Her striking beauty took him completely off his guard. He stuttered his words when she introduced herself after bullying another co-worker named Emily into trading tables. She was confident she would have had the man's undivided attention and bank account balance by the end of the night had Coleman not stalked her with annoying demands like *"hurry up,"* and *"clean that up right now"* and irritating questions every five minutes like *"why is your table still waiting for their food?"* Coleman was a buzzkill in Liza's eyes. She needed to land her "Sugar Daddy" and fast!

"Everyone just... take a break. We regroup back here in twenty," Coleman huffed. He needed the break himself.

Melody approached him as the crowd dispersed. She placed a hand on his tense shoulder. "Coleman, you look a little frazzled. I know this isn't your first wedding. Why do you look like you're the one with wedding jitters?" she asked him. Her voice held a note of concern. "Are you worried the new staff won't be ready?"

"Melody, if I had to list my successes in life, revitalizing this inn would be one of them," he answered her confidently, but then continued. "Securing the right people to run it... well, that's a whole other challenge. In fact, as it stands, it's a borderline failure. I live for the day I have complete faith in my employees."

Just then, Emily Norton, a shy, mousy server, entered the kitchen. She seemed extremely concerned about approaching Coleman. It was as if she was about to give him bad news, even though that was not the case. Melody wondered if Coleman had been stressing the staff to the point where he had become unapproachable.

"Mr. Urquhart, sir, we've finished setting up for the rehearsal dinner in the large parlor," Emily stammered nervously.

"Oh, I highly doubt that, Emily! Did you steam the wrinkles from the linens as I asked?" Coleman asked curtly. He glared at her over his shoulder, not even giving her the courtesy to turn and face her.

Emily lowered her eyes, realizing she had forgotten that one important request from her strict employer. "No... no, sir. I'll get on it right now." Quickly, she left the room to amend her mistake. She cursed herself for forgetting the detail. Even though Coleman was incapable of noticing it now, Emily was his best worker. She worked for the previous owners of the inn for years. She knew every detail of the inn and had the potential to be Coleman's "right hand" if he would just give her a chance. Day in and day out, she tried her best to please him, so forgetting such an important detail made her doubt her own abilities. She cared about the inn and wanted each event to be special for every guest. After all, these events were some of their clients' most important life milestones, and Emily loved helping them make beautiful memories

Coleman looked at the clock, his face visibly frustrated at how fast time was flying. Melody stepped a little closer to him. "Perhaps, softening your tone might help with some of the staff that are trying hard. It looks like they are starting to fear you, Coleman, rather than respect you," Melody said.

"Honestly, I have no time for any level of incompetence. Even the best of intentions does not make a successful event. It's all in the execution, as I'm sure you know well. Now, if you'll excuse me, we're running late." Coleman headed for the refrigerator, where the chef was chatting up Leslie. "Chef! Let's get a move on! Afternoon, Leslie."

Leslie, who had been sharing recipes with the Chef, bade her farewells to him and Coleman. Melody watched as the staff filed back into the kitchen for round two of prep training. Coleman barked more orders.

She sighed. The service business could be a tough occupation with a solid team, let alone without.

"C'mon, Smudge. Time to head out," Melody said as Smudge followed her out of the kitchen. Leslie had gone ahead to start the van.

As Melody and Smudge walked past the large parlor where the rehearsal dinner would be held later that night, Melody paused. The double doors were open, and from the corner of her eye, something caught her attention. Quickly, she back peddled and tucked herself against the wall. Smudge saw Melody's reaction and tucked behind her legs. Melody held a finger against her lips, hinting for Smudge to be quiet.

Inside the parlor, Jared and Liza were in deep conversation. While Melody couldn't hear what their whispered voices were saying, their body language told the story loud and clear. Liza leaned against a wall. She looked up at Jared with a coy expression, her fingers caressed the top of her phone, and she bit her bottom lip suggestively. Jared had a palm against the wall Liza was leaning on, his body directly in front of hers, and somewhat blocking her path. They flirted mercilessly.

When it appeared that Jared was going to lean in and kiss Liza, Melody knew she had to confront them!

CHAPTER THREE

"*M*el! Come! Meet my cousin!" Bradford Smedley spotted Melody flattened against the wall near the parlor entrance. He hadn't realized she was snooping on Jared and Liza through the open doorway, but his voice was loud enough to break up Jared and Liza's flirt fest inside the parlor.

She witnessed them separate quickly. Liza looked around to see if Coleman had spotted them, and Jared immediately pointed his nose at his cellphone to give the appearance that he had been texting. Melody made a mental note to confront Jared at the first opportunity. She wouldn't let him misbehave at

Kerry's wedding, thereby jeopardizing her happy day. At his own wedding, he had made a scene that had Kim in tears. He was rude, obnoxious, and drunk, flirting with one of Kim's bridesmaids. Kerry couldn't help but think their marriage was doomed from the very beginning.

"Nice to meet you, Bradford's cousin," Melody said as she walked toward them. Smudge trotted along at her feet.

Bradford couldn't wait to introduce them. "Maxwell Smedley, meet Melody Marshall. She's one of Kerry's best friends and her business partner. She also made the wedding cake, so when you gain a few pounds from the wedding, you'll know who to thank." Bradford turned to Melody. "Maxwell flew in all the way from Las Vegas to be here!"

Maxwell was a bit older than Bradford. He was well dressed, with a look that was somewhere between a lawyer and a casino manager. Melody couldn't quite tell which was more appropriate, but he looked like he had money to invest in his clothing. He was a sharped dressed man with a designer suit and designer shoes. He was also naturally jovial and had a contagious smile that showed off his perfectly capped teeth. His skin was tanned from the Las Vegas sun.

Bradford had often spoken of Maxwell whenever their group of friends got together. He felt Maxwell was more like a brother than a cousin. Due to both of their work schedules, it was difficult for them to visit with each other. This made Bradford all the more excited that his cousin had come to the wedding.

"That's wonderful! It's a pleasure to meet you, Maxwell. I hope your flight was pleasant enough. That's a long one, isn't it?"

"Indeed it was, but lucky for me, I can sleep anywhere, and I slept the whole way here. The stewardesses also kept me well hydrated, if you know what I mean," he said with a wink.

Smudge yipped a greeting. Always excited to meet new people, her stubby little tail wiggled, and her paws tap-danced against the stone floor. Her little wet nose sniffed toward Maxwell.

"Who's this cutie-pie?" he asked as he pointed at Smudge.

"This is Smudge, my little sweet-face." Melody scooped up Smudge in her arms so Smudge could get a good look at Maxwell. Smudge gave Melody wet kisses along her chin then sniffed at Maxwell again.

He reached out to pet Smudge, but then pulled his hand back quickly and politely as he asked, "May I? I can tell Smudge is a friendly girl, but I don't want to take liberties."

Smudge answered by kissing his fingertips. Melody nodded with an approving smile.

"Oh, yes. She's quite friendly and smart as a whip!"

"She's great. What a beauty! Gorgeous coloring, too." Maxwell scratched Smudge's ear. "And you're quite a beauty, too!" He playfully flirted with Melody.

"C'mon, now, Max. Mel is engaged. Leave the woman alone," Bradford interjected with a grin then went on to brag, "You know, Smudge is a bit of a celebrity here in Port Warren. So, is Mel. She and Mel have helped the Sheriff's Department solve some tricky crimes on several occasions!"

Melody nodded with a smile and brought her hand

up to show off her engagement ring confirming Bradford's engagement news then blushed when he mentioned their sleuthing talents.

"Darn it. All the good ones are taken. Speaking of good ones, I think I'll grab a drink before all the good liquor is gone. I suddenly feel quite thirsty, and if I stick around here too long with these two, they just may consider me a suspect in their next case! See you at dinner, Bradford. Nice meeting you, Melody – and Smudge."

Smudge barked a goodbye as Melody lowered her to the ground. Maxwell headed off, and Melody's eyes followed him curiously. That's when she noticed the reason he was suddenly in need of a beverage. Liza Summers was serving cocktails on a silver tray to arriving guests. Maxwell didn't hesitate to chat with the pretty blond whose hair was now pulled back in a neat bun. He introduced himself and made it a point to let Liza know he'd be in town for a few days.

Liza flashed Maxwell her best smile. By the looks of him, perhaps she had finally found a suitable prospect. After all, Maxwell had no ring on his manicured finger, and Liza could no doubt smell the money burning a hole in his wallet. Melody watched them flirt with each other for a few moments.

"He seems like a character," Melody said to Bradford as she watched Liza coyly pass Maxwell a flute of champagne. He sipped it and put on a show, acting as if it was the best champagne he'd ever tasted ... *because it came from Liza.*

"Max? He talks a good game, but really, he's harmless."

"Do you think he'll cause any trouble at the wedding? Does he drink too much? Get rowdy? Does he handle rejection well?" As far as Melody could tell, Maxwell was laying it on thick to Liza. *What if she spurned his attention?*

"He's not going to cause any trouble. He's just being Maxwell. He's a lover, not a fighter. If she's not interested, he'll peacefully move on to the next pretty girl. He just enjoys flirting." Bradford laughed at the thought of Maxwell being aggressive, unlike Kim's husband, Jared. He knew Melody was protective of Kerry and the wedding. He knew she wanted her friend to have the most magical day possible, but Maxwell wasn't one to worry about. Melody, however, couldn't shake her concern.

"Somehow, trouble does seem to find us, so let's just keep our eyes open. Kerry is already stressed out about her sister and Jared. I don't care much for him. I almost wish he stayed home just so Kerry wouldn't have to stress."

"She and her sister have not been close in a very long time," Bradford said. "I was hoping the wedding would help mend their relationship, but Jared is still in the picture, and he's still a loser, so most likely, it won't. I wish she would drop that bum. She could do so much better."

Melody sighed, thinking about Kerry's concern for her sister.

"I better get going if I'm going to make it back in time for dinner. Alvin is picking me up at seven o'clock." The two hugged briefly, then Melody led Smudge out the front doors. As they headed toward the van, Melody noticed Kim sobbing on a stone bench like the ones scattered around the gardens. She sat with her face in her hands, her shoulders shook softly.

Smudge whined as she looked up at Melody, her

soulful eyes urging Melody to investigate. Melody nodded at Smudge feeling the same way. They couldn't just leave Kim sitting there crying all by her lonesome.

"I guess I'm going to be late for dinner."

CHAPTER FOUR

"Kim? Are you all right?" Melody spoke to her from a few feet away. She didn't want to startle the woman.

"Yes... I'm fine. I'm just having a moment. It's not every day your baby sister gets married." Kim sniffled and quickly wiped her eyes with the back of her hands. She looked over her shoulder at Melody.

Melody didn't believe Kim was crying over Kerry. The two women hadn't been very close over the last few years. Melody suspected Jared had something to do with these tears. Slowly, she approached Kim.

"Mind if I take a seat? We could talk... if you want."

"Sure, it's a free country," Kim said offhandedly. She shrugged her shoulders. She couldn't very well tell Melody to leave her alone, and yet part of her wanted someone to listen. Kim had known Melody as "her sister's friend," but Kerry had always spoken very highly of Melody. Kim envied them both their close friendship and successful business relationship. Kim missed that type of connection in her life. She certainly didn't have it with Jared, her own husband.

Melody sat on the bench next to her. Smudge followed and sat at Melody's feet. For a moment, they all sat there in silence. Kim struggled to get control of her emotions. Finally, she spoke, and when she did, the words just poured from her like a broken dam lets the waters run.

"My marriage is a mess, and there's nothing anyone can do to help. You know, I told Kerry that I hope she and Bradford are as happy as Jared and me. What a joke! After everything she has seen me go through, how could I say such a thing to her? I might as well have cursed their wedding with that kind of 'wish.'" she said sarcastically between tears. "All I really want to tell her... is to run as fast as she can." Kim stared off into the distance, extending her arm in the direction farthest from the inn. Her line of sight followed, and Melody could tell Kim wished she had done the same.

Melody gently touched Kim's arm, guiding it back down to her side.

"Have you ever told Jared how you feel? Maybe, it's time you two had a solid heart to heart. You've been together so long. There's nothing wrong with needing a change." Melody tried to console her. "Kim, *something* has to change."

With a dark laugh, Kim shook her head hopelessly. "If you're suggesting we divorce, that's not a solution, Melody. I know you're not married yet, but it's a lot more difficult than it looks – especially years later. I know everyone thinks he's a bad guy. He wasn't always that way. We've had a lot of good years in between, and no one knows him the way I do. *No one could love him the way I do.* But something has changed for the worse. I don't know how we've gotten so disconnected from each other, and now we're beyond talking, you see how he is. He's rude, and he has such a high opinion of himself, I'm not sure his ego can hear me all the way up there. We can barely stand to be in the same room as each other, and yet, he will not let me leave. Believe me, I've tried."

Kim sniffed again and wiped her eyes. Her tears were done for the time being, and she made an effort to get herself visibly together. "Right now, I just need to get through the next few days for my sister. *I miss her so much, Melody.* I truly wish I could have her back and be close to her again... like how the two of you are." A few straggling tears fell from her eyes.

It was at that moment that Melody noticed Kim had the same eyes as Kerry; only hers were sad and forlorn. Silently, Melody hoped Kerry's eyes would always stay bright, hopeful, and loving.

Melody took Kim's hand in hers. It was a bit awkward since they weren't really friends, but the woman needed one desperately, and Melody was at a loss for words. She let the touch speak for her. Something Kim had said struck a chord in Melody. It was true, she hadn't been married yet, but she liked to think that she and Alvin had a better relationship than what she was witnessing with Kim and Jared. Alvin was nothing like Jared, and Melody couldn't imagine Jared being nice even in his earlier years of marriage to Kim despite what Kim had said. As far as

Melody could remember, Kerry disliked Jared and never had a nice word to say about him.

Kim pulled her hand from Melody's and wiped her eyes again.

"I better let you go. You'll be late for the rehearsal dinner."

As Melody rose from the bench, the Decadently Delicious van pulled up at the curb. Leslie waved from the driver's seat. She gave Melody a concerned look and asked, "Everything ok, here?" Kim forced a wave back at Leslie as she rose from the bench. She took in a deep breath and held it a moment as she turned her face to the sky. The last rays of the day's sun warmed her stinging cheeks. Kim knew she had to get her act together to get through this wedding without ruining it.

"I'm going to see if I can find Jared. I want to clear the air before the wedding. Thanks for the chat, Melody."

Melody had an odd feeling. Typically, when someone unloaded in an emotional outburst, they appeared relieved – like they had gotten their concerns off their chest. But Melody noticed Kim still had that dark, hopeless gaze in her eyes. It was a look that gave Melody a bad feeling about Kim, Jared, and the wedding.

"What was that about?" Leslie asked as Melody loaded Smudge into the van. "Kim looks a little crazy, don't you think?"

"She's having a really hard time with Jared. I think their marriage is finally at a dead end. I just hope they can manage to keep it together until after the wedding. It's the least she can do for her sister and Bradford." Silently, though, Melody wasn't confident that Kim would be able to let her sister have her day. She had a sinking feeling in the pit of her stomach.

CHAPTER FIVE

"Here you go, Smudge." Melody settled Smudge in her large doggy bed along with her favorite stuffed purple elephant. Melody called the elephant "Nelly." Smudge, the brilliant pup she was, knew the toy by name, and when Melody told her to retrieve it, Smudge always got the correct toy. "I'll be back in just a few hours. You be a good girl and watch the house." Melody dropped a kiss on Smudge's little wet nose affectionately. Smudge snuffled at her master, then smothered her face in wet kisses. She turned her attention to Nelly, the elephant, as Melody headed downstairs, where Alvin waited.

"Ooh, la, la! Lady in red!" Alvin's eyes lit up as

Melody descended the staircase. Her red dress fit her figure perfectly. It showed off her curves with classic lines and off the shoulder short sleeves. Her gold slingback high heels accented the dress, and in her hair, she wore a red flower with gold flecks on the petals. Alvin looked equally sharp with his gray suit and black shoes.

"And you, Sheriff Hennessey, are quite dapper!"

"Kerry may not let you sit at her table looking this pretty," Alvin teased. Melody was the most beautiful woman in the world to Alvin. Especially tonight, polished like a ruby, his heart pounded for her. As soon as Melody was within arm's reach, Alvin pulled her in close and dropped a soft kiss just below her ear.

The kiss sent a fantastic shiver down her spine and made her painted toes curl. Yep, Jared was nothing like Alvin, and Melody knew how lucky she was to share her life with a partner like him.

She draped her arms around his shoulders and nuzzled his nose. "Are you going to look this handsome on our wedding day?" she asked with a dreamy look in her eyes.

"It won't matter what I look like on our wedding day. Everyone will be too busy looking at you, Mel." He pressed his lips to hers and held them there for a long, sweet kiss. "But you know I will make every effort to look my best for you."

They shared a second kiss, then drove to the inn. Alvin shared his day's highlights with Melody, such as how Mrs. Caruthers's cat got stuck in a tree again. Melody filled him in on what transpired during the cake delivery.

"I don't understand why the woman keeps letting her cat out. It keeps going up the same tree. Then we keep rescuing it. She should just put a treehouse up there for the cat."

Melody laughed.

"At least, it keeps us busy during downtimes. Maybe she's just lonely and likes the company."

"Not to change the subject, Al, but I'm worried about this wedding. When Leslie and I dropped off the cake this afternoon, Kerry was really stressed about her sister." She took his hand, holding it as he drove down the roadway toward the inn.

"Kim and Jared actually showed? I thought they were estranged."

"They haven't been close in years, but it's because of Jared. Kim basically told me their marriage is over. She was really upset. I don't know how she could possibly get through this wedding without causing a scene. I also saw him flirting with one of Coleman's new hires, a pretty woman named Liza, and it was so blatantly obvious that they were flirting. Then, when they heard Bradford call me, they split up quickly. They looked so suspicious. Between his flirting and Kim's instability, I'm really worried that they're both going to ruin this wedding for Kerry and Bradford."

Alvin squeezed her hand. "Mel, it's going to be fine. I'm sure Kim can find it in her heart to support her sister for one day, and Wilbur and I will keep a steady eye on Jared to make sure he doesn't give her a reason to meltdown and ruin the wedding." Alvin narrowed his eyes on the dark road ahead of them. "I can't imagine living like Jared and Kim. That has to be... tragic."

Melody stared at Alvin in silence for a couple of minutes. He looked at her quickly then turned his eyes back to the road, "What is it, Mel? What are you thinking?" He figured she was thinking about Kim and Jared's sham of a marriage, too.

Mel smiled and leaned in toward Alvin. "I can't wait to marry you, Alvin Hennessey," she whispered in his ear just before pressing her lips to it.

"That's Sheriff Hennessey to you," teased Alvin.

After Alvin parked the car, he escorted his stunningly beautiful date into the inn. Coming back here, he remembered their last visit. Melody had come with Kerry to look at the inn for this very wedding, only a stabbing had occurred, and everything had to be put on hold. Of course, Smudge and Melody had helped him sniff out the clues and solve the murder.

"Why did Kerry come back here... you know, after the stabbing in the inn?" he asked.

"I know, I don't think I would want that memory on my wedding day," Melody said. "The thing is she just loves this place."

"I guess," Alvin said as he pulled the car up and pushed it into park.

Leslie and her date, Wilbur Byrd, were waiting for

them. Wilbur was Alvin's deputy and a good friend. He and Leslie had connected on a more romantic level soon after Melody and Smudge had helped Alvin and Wilbur rescue the puppies of Port Warren. The rescue had made headlines, and Wilbur adopted the two male beagle puppies while Leslie adopted the two females. Their routine puppy playdates blossomed into romantic dates, and now the two were an official "item."

"Hello, gorgeous people!" Leslie said. She wore a brilliant shimmering blue pantsuit with matching high heels. Wilbur wore a blue suit with brown shoes to match. The deputy sheriff cleaned up well. They exchanged greetings all around then entered the large parlor together.

As they sipped cocktails and made small talk, Kerry and Bradford made their entrance into the engagement party. This was an intimate event for the immediate family and the bridal party. Kerry wore a soft, white shift dress. Bradford matched her with a sharp beige suit, a crisp white shirt, and brown shoes. They looked like a celebrity couple straight from the cover of an entertainment magazine. There was a rousing round of applause from their friends and family.

Kerry blushed a deep shade of pink, but she looked so very happy. Bradford gave his future wife a tender peck, which caused the crowd to applaud again. Right on cue, Liza Summers brought over two champagne flutes on a silver platter. Melody felt her eyes narrow on Liza as Bradford picked up both flutes and handed one to Kerry. Melody had not forgotten what she witnessed earlier, and she committed to confronting Liza and Jared at some point that evening. The clock was ticking, and she wanted this event to pass smoothly before the countdown finished.

"To all of our friends and family, joining us near and wide, we thank you for being here and supporting us through this most important milestone. It's really a special time for us, and I'm truly the luckiest man in the world because tomorrow, Kerry Porter will finally be my wife," Bradford said. Then, he looked to the future Mrs. Smedley inviting her to add her own words if she felt so inclined.

The crowd cheered and tapped their utensils against their glasses, creating soft tinkling sounds that mimicked bells. Before Kerry addressed them, she cradled Bradford's face in her hands and placed a tender kiss on his lips. It was an American custom for the happy couple to kiss when their guests made this sound.

"Thank you all for sharing in our happiness. Tomorrow, we, along with the other guests arriving for the wedding, will meet here at two o'clock. We'll exchange our vows just outside the Main Dining Hall, in the large English gardens. Coleman has set up a special area, that's simply breathtaking. Thank you, Coleman." Kerry spotted him in the crowd and blew him a kiss. For the first time in the days leading up to the wedding, Melody noticed Coleman smile.

"After the vows, we'll retire to the Main Dining Hall for the big party!" continued Kerry as she threw her hands up in celebration! "We want all of you to have a great time, and we thank you again for helping Bradford and I make this an affair to remember!"

Midway through the night, sometime after dinner was served but not dessert, Melody excused herself and headed for the ladies' room. The restrooms were located down a narrow hallway, off the open lobby. Further down the same hallway just past the restrooms was an employee entrance to the kitchen.

She left the large parlor, then turned right down a narrow hall. There, just outside the ladies' room door, Emily and Liza argued.

"I know you're stealing my tips, Liza!" Emily said angrily.

"I'm not stealing your tips. I'm just making more than you. I can't help it if my pretty face and charm are worth more than whatever this... is." Liza motioned her hand toward Emily's face and body. "Have you ever been to a salon, or had your eyebrows waxed even once? Maybe contacts instead of glasses?" Her helpful words were delivered with a sarcastic tone.

As Melody walked toward them. Liza stalked off in triumph, rubbing her fingertips together, indicating she was off to make money. Melody glared at her.

"Are you all right?" Melody asked.

"I'd feel better if Liza found another place to work. She's been nothing but trouble since she's been here. Between stealing tips and seducing male guests, she's got a real racket here. Mr. Urquhart is too busy to fully grasp the devil she is." Emily's cell phone alerted her that she had a new text message. "Excuse me, Ms. Marshall I need to answer this – and I apologize for my outburst." Emily headed off to the kitchen.

Melody watched her go then entered the ladies' room to powder her nose.

A few minutes later, Melody emerged from the ladies' room. The kitchen door had opened momentarily as an employee exited. The employee shot her a fretful look that caused Melody to snap her head toward the door. As it slowly swung closed, she saw Coleman berating Emily once again.

This poor girl can't catch a break today.

Coleman can't keep treating his employees this way.

Melody was determined to say something to him.

She headed for the door, and just as she was about to swing it open, her hand recoiled. The sounds of a loud scuffle were coming from the large parlor.

"Oh, no. Here we go!" Melody said as she aborted her kitchen mission and raced to the parlor.

CHAPTER SIX

The large parlor was big enough to host the small engagement party. It was a square room with some cabaret-style tables, a modest dance floor, and a small bar toward the back. A piano player played a selection of songs that held significant meaning for Bradford and Kerry. In the center of the dancefloor, Jared argued with Maxwell, who stood in between Jared and Kim. All three of them had been to the bar on several occasions throughout the night, and the mood was getting tense.

"Hands off my wife, creep!" Jared shouted as he threw a glass at Maxwell's feet, smashing it to pieces.

The room gasped! Jared's outburst interrupting their

conversation, Melody inhaled sharply and rose from her seat. Alvin, Wilbur, and Leslie followed her lead.

"It was just a dance! Like you even care!" Kim yelled from behind Maxwell. Kim was tipsy, her hand cupped around a fresh cranberry and vodka cocktail. "I'm surprised you even noticed. Your eyes have been glued to every pretty young thing in this place since we got here, especially that one!" Unaware of what she was doing, Kim lifted her hand, the cocktail still in it, and pointed it at Liza! Some of the bright reddish-pink liquid splashed toward Liza, spattering her white work shirt. Liza gasped in horror then glared between Jared and Kim before stalking off toward the kitchen to clean herself up.

Before Melody and the team could reach them, Bradford stepped between Jared and Maxwell while Kerry pulled Kim away from the scene. The women naturally split with Melody and Leslie helping Kerry, Alvin and Wilbur jumped in to help Bradford manage Jared and Maxwell.

"I would focus on you if you weren't so self-absorbed and drunk!" Jared yelled after Kim as Alvin and Wilbur yanked him toward the parlor doors.

"Now, listen here, Jared, you shouldn't talk about your wife like that," Maxwell said. "Let's all just calm down and..." But Maxwell never got to finish his sentence. In an instant, Jared broke free from Alvin and Wilbur then slugged Maxwell clumsily in the jaw! Maxwell stumbled back, knocking into Kim, who, as a result, fell into Kerry and spilled the remaining red cocktail all over Kerry's white dress.

Just as Maxwell was about to swing back, Alvin and Wilbur split up, each grabbing a stronger hold on Jared and Maxwell, respectively.

"Break it up! That's enough!" Alvin shouted. "If you two don't quit it, I'll haul both of you down to the station right now." Alvin was so angry; Melody swore she saw steam coming from his nose and ears. Disappointed that Jared and Kim could not keep it together for the sake of Kerry, he glanced darkly toward Melody and shook his head. Melody looked equally angry.

Maxwell pulled his arm free from Wilbur's grip, adjusted his suit. "I don't need this drama. I can get this kind of trouble back in Vegas... *drunk husbands and wives.*" Maxwell hiccupped. "Bradford, Kerry...

I apologize for this disgusting display of machismo. Please excuse me." Then, he stalked off to his room.

"Why must you spoil everything, Kim!" Kerry said. Her hands were shaking out her wet, stained dress.

Kim turned to face her sister; her face contorted with shock over the accusation.

"I... I'm not trying to do anything of the sort, Kerry! I just want to be here for you! You're my sister! I love you!" Kim reached out clumsily to help Kerry wipe her dress. Kerry quickly swatted her hands away, taking a step back from her as if she was repulsed by Kim's presence. A look of disgust darkened her face.

"You're my sister, and you say you love me, yet, you can't help from ruining my wedding? It's my wedding, Kim! Just go," Kerry said with tears brimming in her eyes.

Leslie saw Kerry's face. Quickly, she reached for Kim's arm and pulled her away from Kerry. Melody reached for Kerry and tried to guide her away.

"Maybe you should sleep it off, Kim," Kerry said as she turned away from her.

Kim pulled her arm free from Leslie and snarled at

Melody, "You're not her sister. I am!" It was clear Kim's estrangement from her sister was taking a toll. She looked around the room. Everyone was staring at her. The embarrassment was overwhelming. She wiped her tears with the back of her hand and delicately set down her now empty glass on a nearby table as if to set herself apart from Jared's earlier glass smash. "I'm going to my room," she said calmly as she lifted her chin.

Kim made every attempt to walk out of the room with her head held high, but deep inside, she knew she had destroyed her sister's party and cast a dark shadow on tomorrow's wedding.

"I knew this would happen. I knew it! I should have never invited them to my wedding. This is only the rehearsal dinner, imagine what they will do tomorrow!" Kerry said as she watched Kim leave the parlor.

"Tomorrow will be perfect." Melody took Kerry's hands, trying to reassure her. "Don't worry, we will all make sure that these three behave or go home. Everyone will be watching them and trust me, no one is going to let them give a repeat performance."

"If I have to call in the entire Port Warren Sheriff's Department just to manage crowd control, I'll do it," Alvin said, reinforcing Melody's statement.

"So now, our wedding is going to be a militarized occasion?" Kerry shook her head. She didn't want that at all.

Alvin and Melody shook their heads and tried to soothe Kerry, but it was no use. Melody understood. How could Kim do this?

Bradford pushed through their circle of friends and took his future wife's hand in his. "No. That's not going to happen. Everything will be fine. I'll talk to Maxwell and Jared tonight and make sure they fully understand that I will personally uninvite all of them. In the meantime, let's enjoy the rest of the evening. We haven't even had Mel's cake yet!" His voice was calm and in control as he tried to refocus Kerry on the party.

"But my dress... "

"Kerry, you could make a potato sack look like a Ralph Lauren. Ignore it, and let's dance."

Bradford always knew how to make Kerry smile. She

took his hand as he led her to the dancefloor. The piano player played one of their favorite tunes, and they danced like they were the only two people in the room.

The rest of the party proceeded without incident. Most of the guests were relieved that Jared and Kim didn't return. When the event finally concluded, and all said their goodbyes, Melody and Alvin walked hand in hand out the inn's front doors.

"Wait here, Mel. I'll go get the car."

As Melody waited for Alvin, she noticed two shadowy figures locked in an embrace. They were kissing with passion and abandonment while she tried to identify them. Alvin pulled up and ushered her in the passenger seat.

As he drove past, Liza stepped out of the shadows and into the moonlight. Whomever she was with pulled her playfully back into the shadows for another kiss.

I hope that's not Jared, Melody thought.

CHAPTER SEVEN

*T*he wedding day had finally arrived! The sun was shining with clear blue skies. The gardens were vibrant with color. The fresh day wiped the slate clean on the previous night's drama.

"We're going to be late! Alvin, are you ready?" Melody was slipping into her blush-colored bridesmaid dress. With the back open, she hurried into the bathroom, where Alvin was patting aftershave on his face and neck.

"Mmhmm, you smell good, Al. Zip me, please," Melody said as she spun around, offering him her back.

"Thank you. And if you keep getting dressed up like

this, I'm going to have to marry you." Alvin wiped his hands before he zipped up Melody's dress.

"You have to marry me anyway. You already said yes." Melody saw that twinkle in Alvin's eye. She knew he was remembering the moment when she, unconventionally, proposed to him. He had had every intention of proposing to Melody, but she beat him to it, and he loved her for it.

"Saying yes to you was the smartest thing I've ever done."

Melody gave him a quick peck before heading down the steps. There would be plenty of time to reminisce after Kerry and Bradford were married and off honeymooning. Once this wedding was past them, Melody vowed to plan hers with Alvin. It was time.

"Smudge!"

Smudge trotted to Melody from the kitchen. Fresh from the groomer, her blue-gray coat shined and smelled of Juniper Breeze, a conditioning spray Smudge particularly liked. Smudge had a lifetime supply of it thanks to her part in solving a case involving the puppies of Port Warren. Being a hot news story, it earned media coverage for the product's manufacturer.

"This color really highlights your eyes, Smudge." Melody tied a large, pretty pink bow around Smudge's neck. The soft pale pink complimented her unique blue-gray fur. "You're going to be the prettiest flower pup ever."

Without hesitation, the trio drove out to Bronwyn's Country Inn. Once inside, Melody and Smudge parted ways with Alvin and headed toward Kerry's bridal suite. Alvin joined the other groomsmen in the parlor.

"It's finally here, Mel! After today, I will officially be Mrs. Bradford Smedley, the First!" Kerry grinned as Melody opened the door to the suite.

"The first, huh?" teased Leslie as she zipped up the back of Kerry's white wedding gown.

"Well, I think it has a nice ring to it, don't you?" Kerry asked.

"Indeed, it does. I love it, and I'm so happy for you both," Leslie said with a bright smile. She knew how important this day was for Kerry, and Kerry looked like a bride right out of a magazine.

Kim emerged from the bathroom. Melody glanced at her. She was a bit surprised to see her. Kim offered her a polite smile. Thankfully, Kim was dressed, and if it weren't for her puffy eyes, indicating that she'd had a rough night, it was almost as if the fight didn't happen. None of the women spoke of it, and Kerry seemed to be in good spirits.

"Kerry, let's get your veil on. The photographer should be here shortly." Leslie guided Kerry to the full-length mirror. Seeing the beautiful bride, Smudge barked happily.

"I'd like to touch up her eye makeup before you do that, Leslie. I have this deep shade of blue that I think would make her eyes pop," Kim said.

"I don't want to look like a clown, Kim." Kerry didn't look too happy.

"No, no – just a smudge to create a little contrast."

"Oh – speaking of Smudge! Doesn't she look pretty? Mel, that bow is perfect for her. Thank you both for doing this. Thank you all!" Kerry was beaming with excitement, just the way it should be.

While Leslie helped Kerry with her veil, Melody pulled Kim aside. "Have you spoken with your husband since last night?"

Kim's puffy eyes with dark circles under them narrowed at the mention of her husband.

"Let me tell you about my good for nothing, carousing husband..." Kim said as she started to bring Melody up to speed. But, as Melody hushed her to keep her voice down, a blood-curdling scream suddenly pierced the air!

"Oh, no!" Kerry cried. She knew it was too good to be true. As far as she was concerned, her wedding day was jinxed.

"Everyone! Stay here! Smudge, come!" Melody pulled open the bridal suite door and raced to the lobby where a crowd was already forming. Smudge ran right behind her.

Where did the scream come from? Melody asked herself. With the open lobby of the inn, it was hard to tell.

Smudge knew! Her hearing being more sophisticated. She ran ahead of Melody and led the way toward the kitchen! Melody followed her.

The crowd had started to block the narrow hallway that led toward the employee entrance. Melody pushed her way through it. Smudge deftly navigated the gathering guests' legs and barked at the kitchen door willing it to open.

Together they busted through the door to see Emily sobbing uncontrollably behind one of the kitchen counters. She pointed at the floor, horrified by something inside one of the open cupboards. Coleman was trying desperately to calm her.

"Melody, you don't want to see this. Please, go back outside. Alvin and Wilbur are on their way over. I just sent the chef to get them from the parlor," Coleman's voice was close to breaking.

His warning didn't thwart Melody and Smudge from approaching, though. Smudge whined as she sniffed the cupboard. Melody gently guided Smudge back so she could get a better look. There, stuffed inside, was Liza Summer's strangled body still wearing her white work shirt now stained reddish pink from the splashes from Kim's cranberry cocktail drink. Melody noticed something odd about the body. Instead of Liza's lips being bluish in color, they were also stained a bright red.

"That doesn't make sense. Why would her lips be red?" asked Melody aloud, but not really loud enough for anyone but Smudge to hear. Smudge whined again.

"I swear, Melody, this inn is cursed. It's one bad luck omen after another!" Coleman said, more shakily than ever. He grabbed the sobbing Emily by the arms and shook her. "Get a hold of yourself!" To Melody, Coleman sounded like he was the one that needed to get a grip. The man was nearly hysterical.

"Melody! Are you ok? Where's Smudge?" Alvin asked frantically as he pushed his way through the crowd and into the kitchen. Wilbur was right behind him.

"We're fine! Smudge is here!"

Melody scooped her up and carried her away from the cupboard to make room for Alvin. Soon the sheriff's deputies would arrive and thoroughly investigate the scene, but for now, Alvin initially investigated the body and the cupboard while Wilbur secured the area.

"Alvin," Melody called, "what am I going to tell Kerry?"

He sighed deeply, not having an answer, and their eyes met. It was just a moment, but his strength calmed her. He rubbed his chin as he considered the options. There were none. "Unfortunately, she's going to have to postpone the wedding, and no one is going to be able to leave the property."

After Wilbur secured the area, he approached Coleman and Emily. "Coleman, we need to question everyone, staff, guests, everyone. Let's get them gathered in the parlor. The sooner we get some answers, the sooner Bradford and Kerry can get married. Does anyone have an idea of who might have wanted to see this girl dead?"

Melody looked at Emily suspiciously.

Was the girl's sobbing a genuine reaction, or was she overcompensating to throw them off her scent? Could the dead woman's thievery have been enough to push the surviving waitress too far?

CHAPTER EIGHT

"*I* have to call my wedding off?" Kerry looked confused. A look of shock and horror contorted her pretty face. She sat on the edge of the bed between Melody and Kim, shaking her head. "I guess I knew something would go wrong... with Jared and Kim present... but call off the entire wedding?!"

"Kerry, a woman is dead," Leslie's tone was a touch stern as she tried to explain the seriousness of the situation to her friend. "I know this day is important, but I don't think we should be flippant about the circumstances."

Kerry looked at Leslie, her eyes narrow and dark.

Melody suspected Kerry was about to give Leslie a piece of her mind, so she distracted her quickly.

"Maybe not call off the wedding entirely, but simply postpone – *hopefully not more than a few hours.* I know it's a lot to take in, but Alvin and Wilbur are down there investigating now. I'm going to get an update. Maybe Smudge and I can help them find some answers quickly. I promise, Kerry, we'll crack this case as soon as possible."

Kim took Melody's place beside Kerry once she got up and wished Melody good luck. She and Leslie stayed with Kerry while Melody and Smudge headed back down to the lobby.

By now, the news of Liza Summer's murder had trickled through the guests. Bradford and Maxwell attempted to keep the guests calm while deputies sealed off the building.

"Bradford!" Melody called over the chaos of the crowd.

Bradford finished talking with a great aunt who had traveled a great distance to come to this "great" wedding that had now turned into a murder mystery event. Part of him believed she was more excited about the murder mystery than the wedding. He turned his attention to Melody.

"I really need to be with Kerry. She's probably a mess right now," Bradford said.

"I just left her. Kim and Leslie are both with her. She's upset, but this isn't exactly something anyone could control. I'm going to see if Smudge and I can help move this along." Melody and Smudge shared a well-earned reputation for being amateur sleuths. Surely, she could use this talent to help her friends.

Alvin spotted the two in the lobby and pulled Melody aside. Smudge followed.

"Ok, pastry chef turned Nancy Drew, what are your thoughts? See anything unusual that I should know about?" Alvin asked quietly. He didn't want anyone to hear their conversation.

"I have several thoughts. Yesterday, when I went to the ladies' room, I overheard Liza and Emily arguing. Emily accused Liza of stealing her tips. Liza insulted Emily's looks. She had a real stuck-up way about her. Coleman also didn't care much for Liza, though I'm not sure it's enough to kill her. She was disruptive, and he was frustrated with her."

"Interesting. I'll start with them. Didn't you say something about seeing Jared with Liza, too?"

"Yes! I saw them flirting intensely in the parlor before the party started, and last night when we left, I saw her kissing someone in the shadows."

"You know for sure it was her? Who was she kissing?"

"I'm not sure. The man stayed in the shadows. I couldn't see his face, but there was a moment when Liza stepped into the moonlight, so I know it was definitely her."

"Good work, Mel. Anything else?"

"Yes, one more thing. Emily said that Liza steals tips and flirts with the male guests. She said, 'she has a real racket going on here.' Sounds like Liza was some kind of con artist looking for a meal ticket."

Alvin gave his fiancé a kiss of thanks. He knew he could count on her. "You know, Mel, you would have made an excellent detective."

"You know, Al, if I ever get tired of baking the best cupcakes in Port Warren, I know where to apply. I've got connections."

"That you do."

With the inn shut down and no one allowed to enter or leave, Wilbur and the deputies kept the guests in check while they processed the scene thoroughly. Alvin converted Coleman's private office into an interrogation room. It was Emily's turn to give a statement.

"Emily, we need to understand your relationship with Liza," Alvin said. "What can you tell us?"

"Liza was far from my favorite person. I'm not happy she's dead, but I can't say I'm surprised, either." Emily now appeared quite composed and over the initial shock of seeing Liza's dead body. "She was a bad person. She used a lot of people to get what she wanted, and she never really cared about doing a good job."

Suddenly realizing she may be a suspect, Emily added, "If I were going to kill her, I would have gotten rid of the body in a far cleverer fashion. I've seen CSI, and I'm very organized. Mr. Urquhart can verify my performance – even though sometimes he seems unhappy with it." Emily continued to tell Sheriff Hennessey all about Liza's downfalls. She revealed how Liza never listened to Mr. Urquhart, who Emily felt worked tirelessly to make the inn a success. She explained how Liza had no respect for the inn, Mr. Urquhart, or the other staff members, often stealing their tips. Lastly, she explained how Liza would flirt with the male guests to get gifts or money from them. "She wasn't an aspiring model or actress; she was an aspiring freeloader and con artist."

Alvin concluded the interview for the time being but advised Emily not to go anywhere.

Coleman, who had been listening in on the interrogation, suddenly had a change of heart toward Emily. He was impressed with her assessment of Liza's performance and finally noticed Emily had only the best intentions for the inn and its success. When Alvin left the private office to check in with Wilbur, Coleman grabbed his attention.

"Sheriff! I'd like to make a statement," Coleman said.

"I'll be interviewing you shortly, Coleman. You sure it can't wait?" Alvin asked as he paused in his steps to give the proprietor his full attention.

"Well, it's about Emily. Emily may have hated Liza, but she's always taken the high road. She's a strong, valuable employee that always puts the business before her own needs. I can see her reporting Liza. She's done that, but I can't see her murdering Liza. Emily is a professional, not a psycho. In fact, I should appreciate her work ethic and talent more."

"Thank you for your input, Coleman. Let me check in with my team, and then we'll talk more."

Alvin excused himself to reconvene with Wilbur and Melody. He told them about Emily's interview.

"I kind of agree with Coleman. Emily works very hard. I can't see her snapping and killing Liza over tip money. Could it really be enough money to risk prison? I don't think so," Melody rationalized, Smudge barked. Melody was not sure if it was in agreement or to get attention. Alvin gave her ears a quick rub anyway.

Alvin and Wilbur both nodded in agreement, but they all knew that people had committed murder over less.

"We need to find out who else has a motive," Wilbur said. "She was strangled. It could very well be a crime of passion. Jared and Maxwell fit the bill. Maybe she was trying to play both of them for money – and maybe she was using them to make the other one jealous." He shrugged to the others.

"Maybe Maxwell found out she was trying to take advantage of his money and strangled her in a drunken rage?" Alvin questioned.

"I'm not sure. Bradford made it crystal clear that Maxwell is a lover and not a fighter. He told me that if Liza rejected him, he'd just move on," Melody added.

"Rejected and being swindled are two different things," Alvin said, and they all nodded.

At that moment, Bradford approached them. Melody studied Bradford's face. He was visibly tired and stressed. It occurred to her that here they were focusing on "Kerry's big day" when it was just as much Bradford's big day.

He must be so disappointed, she thought.

"Sorry to interrupt, but could you guys come upstairs? My cousin, Maxwell, has something he wants to confess."

CHAPTER NINE

*A*lvin, Wilbur, Melody, and Smudge followed Bradford to a guest room on the second floor. There, they found Maxwell sitting in a chair by the window nursing a drink. He didn't look nearly as put together as he did when he first arrived at the inn. In this light, Melody could see the dark circles that pooled under his eyes. He had fine lines etched in the corners of his eyes, laugh lines or worry lines. His clothes looked wrinkled and dingy. They were the same clothes he wore to the engagement party. She hadn't recalled seeing him downstairs at all that day. *Had he been hiding up here this entire time? Was he capable of killing the pretty but shady server?*

"Maxwell. Bradford said you have something to confess regarding the dead woman downstairs?" Alvin said sternly.

Maxwell looked up at Alvin as his hand pulled the shade closed. The light had been bothering his eyes, or he felt he could tell his story better in the dark. "Yes, Sheriff," Maxwell said. "I knew Liza *intimately*. I met her during the early afternoon of the rehearsal dinner... yesterday. We shared a few intimate moments and made plans to meet again after the dinner. I'm telling you this because you may find evidence that places her in my room." His hand motioned around the room they currently occupied.

"Except after dinner, when she was supposed to be meeting me, I saw her outside kissing someone else." Maxwell took a swig of his drink, held it in his mouth for a moment then swallowed hard.

"What happened next? Did you confront her?" Alvin asked.

"Well, if you all hadn't noticed, I had a little too much to drink. I'm pretty sure she was kissing that moron, Jared. I waited for her to come back inside, and then, yeah, I confronted her. I'll blame it on the liquor, but I got rude and even called her a few names I probably shouldn't have. She got mad and stormed off toward the kitchen. I followed her into the kitchen, we argued some more, but then I felt sick. I felt *really* sick like I was going to blackout."

The seconds stretched as Maxwell looked down at his glass.

"Do you think it's possible you killed her, Max?" Alvin asked.

Max drained his glass as he thought about it.

"Do I think I could have killed her? No. But I blacked out. I don't remember anything after seeing her in the kitchen. If I could have done it, we should find out. Right, Bradford?" His tone was filled with venom. "Maybe if we can wrap this up, Bradford and Kerry can still get married. That's all that's on his mind right now, anyway. Kerry, Kerry, Kerry." It was clear Max was still a little drunk and unsure of himself, and he was resenting Bradford for pressuring him to speak to the sheriff when he wasn't even sober yet.

"Max, it's our wedding day! Of course, I'm

concerned about my wife. Her dream wedding was just destroyed, and I really hope you had nothing to do with it!" Bradford was beyond frustrated.

"All right, enough. Wilbur, please take Maxwell into custody and get his prints. We'll find out soon enough if there's something to be worried about here," Alvin ordered.

Wilbur took Max by the arm and escorted him downstairs. Bradford looked helpless.

"I just want to figure out whodunit so I can marry Kerry. We have been waiting for this moment for a long time. I just want her to officially be my wife, and Maxwell is like my brother. I really hope he wasn't involved in this. It's hard enough on Kerry being estranged from her sister. She loves Max just as much as I do," Bradford explained.

Melody sat next to him. Smudge snuffled his ankles, sat on his feet, and then leaned her body against his leg affectionately.

"I know, Bradford, and it will happen," Melody reassured him. "If Max had an encounter with Liza, and Emily said she did this repeatedly, maybe there is another guest in addition to Jared and Maxwell that she burned."

"We still need to locate Jared and question him. No one has seen him since last night. We need to find out if he was the one kissing Liza last night."

Just then, Kim entered the room, crying.

CHAPTER TEN

"I need to speak to Sheriff Hennessey," Kim said urgently, her eyes teary. They all looked up at her suspiciously.

"What did you do?" Bradford asked as he stood up quickly, his hands balled into fists and he glared at her.

"Bradford! Go check on Kerry. Let us talk with Kim privately," Alvin said, guiding the angry man out of the room. Once Bradford was in the hall, Alvin shut the door and turned his attention back to Kim.

He extended his hand to offer her a seat on the bed. Kim sat down. Her tears flowed, and she became incoherent.

"Kim, we need to find Jared. No one has seen him since last night. Do you know where he is or anything about Liza's death?" Melody asked gently. "Please, Kim? We need to resolve this case as soon as possible."

Kim took a breath and steadied her voice.

"After the fight last night, I went back to my room. From the window, I saw Jared outside. He was so angry! When he gets riled up, there's no stopping his rage until he indulges his basic instincts and takes his anger out on something or someone, usually me." She pulled up one of the sleeves of her dress and showed them bruises in the shape of fingerprints embedded in her arm.

"Kim, I'm so sorry that you have been married to this monster for so long!" Melody was enraged by the marks on Kim's arm.

"I didn't want to ruin her wedding by telling her that Jared was putting his hands on me. She already hates me, and after this, she'll never speak to me again – I'm sure of it!" Kim stopped, overcome with tears once more.

Melody went to Kim's side to console her as she continued her story.

"I could see him outside, kicking bushes and knocking over cigarette cans. He even kicked the side of someone's car. He was completely enraged. Then, I saw someone walking toward him. It was Liza. She was consoling him, trying to calm him. She kissed him! But that's when I saw Maxwell arguing with them. He was drunk and calling Liza names. Then, they all disappeared inside." Kim stopped abruptly, giving her audience time to think.

"Stay here, Kim. We need to find Jared and get to the bottom of this – and we're not done discussing your domestic violence situation. Please, stay here and lock the door," Alvin said just before he, Melody, and Smudge left her to find Jared.

As the three headed back down to the main lobby, Alvin called Wilbur.

"If you see Jared Anders, you are to detain him immediately. He's a primary person of interest. Kim's story lines up with Maxwell's except for a few details that could be skewed due to them both being intoxicated. The stories are close enough for us to loom at Jared. I think Jared followed them back into the inn. When Maxwell blacked out or left, Jared snuck into the kitchen and killed Liza, probably in a jealous, drunken rage."

"Got it, Chief. I think I saw him trying to get back into the inn earlier. I'll go see what I can find out," Wilbur said.

Jared was indeed trying to enter the inn, but a deputy monitoring the entrance was refusing him entry.

"I'm telling you, I'm a guest here. My wife is inside. It's my sister-in-law's wedding," Jared explained. The deputy did not deviate from his strict orders. No one was to enter or leave the inn until the sheriff cleared the building.

"Let him in, Deputy," Alvin ordered. Melody and Smudge stood behind him, watching.

The deputy stepped out of the way, and Jared gave him a smug look as if he had a special pull in the joint, only to find Alvin was ready to arrest him.

"Jared Anders, you're under arrest for spousal abuse, and you're now a suspect in the murder of Liza

Summers. You will be read your rights and taken down to the station for processing." Sheriff Hennessey called for backup deputies to arrest Jared.

"Wait! What? I did no such thing – on both counts! I never laid a hand on my wife, and I definitely did not kill Liza ... wait – who is Liza Summers?" Jared protested.

Wilbur grabbed Jared's other arm, ready to put him in cuffs, but something in Jared's reaction made Alvin pause. "Take him to the office. We'll question him here." They dragged him inside.

"**O**k, Jared. As a courtesy to your sister-in-law and your wife, we're going to give you the opportunity to tell us the truth," Alvin said. "Start talking."

"I'm telling the truth! I was so pissed off last night, I left here, drove around, and rented a room at the Port Warren motel." Jared paused. "You know, I don't have to talk to you. I can lawyer up if I want."

"Sounds like a convenient admission, Anders," Alvin

said. "We have a witness that shows you destroying property, and your wife has bruises all up and down her arm. We also have witnesses that place you with Liza before your outburst during the rehearsal dinner and kissing her outside after the dinner. You two had the hots for each other, right? Maybe she changed her mind and rejected you. Maybe she chose Maxwell. Who's to say you didn't lose your temper with her, too? Wilbur, take this wife-beater down to the station. He makes my stomach turn."

As Wilbur slapped a cuff on one of Jared's wrists, Jared pleaded for him to wait. "Ok! Ok! I was outside with some blond, but she kissed me! I didn't kiss her, and then Max came out yelling at her. The two of them went inside, and that's when I left and drove around. I didn't touch that girl!"

"Take him away, Wilbur, and hold him there until I finish up here. I'm sure we're going to find the evidence we need to convict you, Anders. You can kiss all your girlfriends goodbye when I send you to prison."

Wilbur finished cuffing Jared and dragged him outside the office where Kim and Kerry were waiting.

"What did you tell them, Kim? Did you tell them you're a drunk and a liar, too?" Jared spat as Wilbur dragged him along.

Kim watched the deputies take her husband away. She was speechless. Kerry put her hand on Kim's shoulder. Kim spun to face her.

"Kerry, I'm so very sorry. I swear I had no desire to disrupt your wedding or steal the spotlight or anything like that." Kim's eyes were swollen from the tears she shed over the last two days.

Kerry exhaled softly. Seeing her sister's arm, she realized there were more important issues now than the wedding.

"It's ok. Bradford and I spoke about it. A murder is a pretty serious reason to postpone a wedding, and I'm really worried about you, Kim. Bradford and I can get married anytime. We're already married in our hearts. We're prepared to be there for you. You need both of us right now." Kerry took Kim into her arms and gave her a tight hug. Bradford joined in, hugging them both.

But something still didn't feel right. Melody and

Smudge looked at each other. *Was this case really solved?*

Neither of them was convinced. Melody looked at Smudge. "Something is not right. There's still no real proof that Jared went into the kitchen. I'm sure someone at the motel can confirm he slept there – if he's telling the truth. C'mon Smudge, let's go do some sleuthing. I've got my own suspicions."

CHAPTER ELEVEN

Smudge followed Melody back to the kitchen, where the coroner was taking Liza's body away. She waited for him to finish and then discreetly let Smudge roam, knowing the little Frenchie would sniff out any important clues.

Inside the kitchen, Emily collected cleaning supplies. She wanted to clean the crime scene so the inn could get back to business. Coleman Urquhart was surveying the crime scene.

"Emily, you shouldn't touch anything yet. Even though the body has been removed, it's still a crime scene," Melody explained. From the corner of her eye, Melody spotted Smudge, the little sleuth, sniffing the cupboard. At first, her sniffing was casual, but then it intensified as if she was picking up a scent. Smudge was small enough to fit in the cupboard, so she burrowed deeper inside to investigate. Melody kept a watchful eye on Smudge even though she continued her conversation with Emily.

"I... I was hoping to get everything cleaned up. Maybe we could still have the wedding. I feel so bad for Bradford and Kerry. I know this day meant a lot to them." Emily held a bucket in one hand and a mop in the other.

"I know, but they have decided to postpone the wedding indefinitely," Melody said.

Smudge was snuffling loudly as she nosed around in the cupboard. She hadn't moved onto another location, so she was definitely onto something.

"Oh, no!" Coleman said, imagining the deafening silence of an empty cash register in his head.

Noticing Smudge was belly deep in the cupboard, Melody excused herself from her conversation with Emily and guided Smudge gently from the cupboard. "What did you find, Smudge? Let me see, girl."

Much to Melody's surprise, Smudge's snout was covered in a red sticky substance, but it looked familiar!

"Smudge, is that frosting on your nose?" Melody touched her fingertip to the red substance and sniffed it. She knew that faint lemon scent! She also recognized the color since she made it in the bakery! The red substance was colored just like the red roses Melody applied to Kerry's wedding cake, and when she touched her tongue to it, Melody knew she'd recognize that taste anywhere. Smudge also enjoyed licking it off her nose.

Coleman spotted Smudge's nose and recognized the red coloring as well. He knew he had seen it before and quickly headed to the refrigerator where Melody's cake was stored, only to find a chunk had been torn out!

"Melody! Look at this!" Coleman wheeled the rolling cart out of the refrigerator. "Liza must have helped herself to a snack before her untimely demise."

"Yes! I noticed her lips were unusually bright red when we first discovered the body! Normally, they would have been blue," Melody said, realizing that she had seen too many bodies to know this.

"That doesn't make any sense at all," Emily said. Melody and Coleman looked to her for an explanation.

"You said yourself that she was a thief and had no respect for the inn, Coleman or her employees," Melody said.

Emily nodded and replied to Melody, "Yes, I know, but she also abhorred sweets. Liza valued her looks above all else. She knew her face and figure were her moneymakers. She wouldn't risk damaging them for anything and certainly not for a piece of cake. She was intensely vain. If she ate that cake, she was forced to eat it."

CHAPTER TWELVE

*M*elody and Smudge updated Alvin about Smudge's discovery, then went to Kerry's room to check in on her. There, they found Kerry and Kim talking.

"How are you both holding up?" Melody asked.

Kerry rose from the bed and guided Melody outside the room. She shut the door behind them since she wanted to talk to her privately. Smudge stayed inside, giving Kim sweet kisses and cuddles.

"I may have to take a leave of absence at the bakery to help my sister. I'm going to go home with her and try to help her sort through this mess with Jared. Who knows how long this investigation could last?

I'm not sure Kim can handle it on her own," Kerry said.

"Of course. You need to be there for your family. There's still a chance Jared didn't kill Liza, but those marks on your sister's arm still need to be addressed."

Together, they entered the room again. Kim came out of the bathroom, leaving the door open behind her. Melody noticed that Smudge was sniffing around the room intently.

"I think it's great that Kerry will be going home with you, Kim. It's great you two are reconnecting, unfortunately over these circumstances, but still," Melody said, making conversation even though her eyes were still on Smudge, who was now sniffing around Kim's suitcases. It looked as if Kerry had been helping Kim pack.

"Do you really believe Jared could have killed Liza?" Melody asked.

"Do you really think he's didn't? You witnessed his behavior yourself. There's no way I could live with what he's done, especially now that he's ruined my sister's wedding."

"Right, your sister's wedding," Melody repeated. Her response made Kim defensive.

Smudge disappeared into the bathroom, still sniffing. *What could she be looking for?* Melody wondered.

"What are you implying, Melody?" Kim asked. There was something in Melody's tone that irked her. Kim pulled back her sleeve again, reminding Melody of what Jared was capable of, but the marks on Kim's arm looked drastically improved. The bruises which were much darker were now very faint. *Could they be fake? After all, Kim had plenty of time alone to apply them with that deep blue makeup.*

"Did you not see these the first time? You think I just wanted to destroy my sister's wedding?" Kim was getting increasingly agitated and defensive.

"Oh, I didn't say anything of the sort!" Melody held up her hands submissively. "But now that you mention it..." Melody was sure Jared was guilty of something, but not necessarily murder and possibly not assault. There was something about the way Kim came forward that she distrusted. As she was about to dig deeper, Smudge interrupted her.

Smudge barked, but it was muffled. She stood

behind Kim, holding something in her mouth. The three women turned to look at the pup. Melody suddenly knew exactly what it was!

In her mouth was the dress that Kim wore to the rehearsal dinner, but today it was covered with Kerry's wedding cake, including some of the red rose icing!

"Nice work, Smudge!" Melody nodded.

Kim lunged for the dog, trying to grab the dress from her mouth, but Smudge was too fast and ran around the room, keeping a hold of it.

Kerry stepped between Smudge and her sister. She was furious! Melody blocked the door and quickly summoned Alvin via text!

"How dare you," Kerry hissed. "You always had to have center stage. You were like this when we were kids, and you're like this now. Nothing has changed! Let's see how being the center of attention in prison works out for you!"

CHAPTER THIRTEEN

"*I*'m not lying! Jared is abusive! He's the one you want!" Kim cried as Wilbur led her through the front lobby in handcuffs.

"No one doubts he's abusive, Kim. We've seen him be unkind, but that doesn't make him a murderer. You may have gotten away with blaming him had you not stuffed Kerry's wedding cake in your victim's mouth," Melody said. "You just had to destroy that, too!"

Kim snarled at Melody from over her shoulder and shoved Wilbur back on his feet. She was at her breaking point and apparently quite strong! Adrenaline could do that to a person. This confirmed Kim was capable of overpowering Liza.

"I saw them kissing outside the inn! Liza thought she was so powerful; she thought she could have any man she wanted with her pretty face and young, perfect body. It gave me the greatest pleasure stuffing that cake down her throat!" Kim admitted. The anger was oozing from her very being.

Emily and Coleman watched the scene. Remembering something important, Emily ran up to Melody quickly and showed her a text she received during the rehearsal dinner. It was the same text she received when she excused herself from her conversation with Melody outside the ladies' room.

"She asked me to give her a tour of the kitchen! She must have been planning how she was going to murder Liza!" Emily said.

"The cost of murder just went up, Kim!" Alvin said. "That's premeditation right there."

CHAPTER FOURTEEN

A few days later, Coleman Urquhart and Emily Norton dropped by Decadently Delicious to meet with Bradford and Kerry.

"Thank you for meeting with us," Emily said on behalf of herself and Coleman.

Melody and Smudge hung back to give the four privacy.

"We would really appreciate the opportunity to host your wedding, again," Coleman said. "We've made some significant changes in staff, and Emily has been promoted to my assistant manager. I'm finally confident we have the right team in place to make the inn the success it deserves to be, and your wedding would be a great opportunity for us to prove it to you and to Port Warren."

Kerry took Bradford's hand and looked into his eyes, before replying to Coleman and Emily. Bradford nodded for Kerry to tell them their news. Bradford and Kerry had also made some significant changes in their wedding plans.

"We appreciate you coming to the shop to talk with us, but Bradford and I have decided to go another route. We've decided to keep our wedding more intimate. We don't need an elaborate affair. We realized how much pressure having the perfect wedding put on both of us. We don't want to start our new life together, stressed, and worried about what could go wrong. We just need each other. That's all that matters. We do wish you luck with the inn, and we're happy to hear the inn that's been such an important part of Port Warren's history will still be an important part of its future - and who knows, maybe one day a baby shower at the inn will be in our future."

"Do you mean...?" Emily asked.

Kerry and Bradford both laughed.

"No! Not yet. First things first, but one day." Kerry gave Bradford's hand a gentle squeeze.

"Well, I can't say I'm not disappointed. Your wedding was going to be one of our best yet, but I understand, considering the circumstances," Coleman said sadly.

Once Emily and Coleman left, Melody approached Kerry and Bradford.

"I hope you two aren't scrapping your wedding plans altogether," she said.

Kerry and Bradford exchanged a secretive look and laughed.

"Nope, we're actually headed to Las Vegas! Isn't it romantic? It's like eloping, and Maxwell has promised to show us a good time!" Kerry was over the moon with excitement. Bradford laughed and hugged her.

"And, we have some more news," Bradford said. "We want you, Alvin and Smudge, to join us and be our witnesses at the Elvis Chapel O' Love!"

How could Melody resist an offer like that?

Smudge yipped and spun excitedly while Melody speed-dialed Alvin.

"I'll call Alvin right now! Smudge, get ready for a cross-country trip!"

If you enjoyed this book Grab Smudge and the Stolen Puppies FREE when you join my newsletter here

Read on for an amazing offer

Grab the first 6 books in the Bakers and Bulldogs series in this box set for FREE with Kindle Unlimited here or read on for the preview.

Ding. Melody stretched the dough a little further; holding her breath as she expertly pulled it just enough to ensure a perfectly thin, translucent layer. The bell pinged again, and Melody glanced around for Kerry.

"Hey, Ker—where are you?" she called, failing to detect her assistant's presence. Melody shook her head, wiped her hands on her apron, exited the kitchen and hurried into the shop. There stood her best customer, Alvin Hennessy, the small town's local sheriff, his kind brown eyes lighting up as Melody came into his view. He hastily removed his hat, cleared his throat and smiled sheepishly down at her.

"Oh, hey there, Mel. Sorry to stop in again today, but I forgot I needed a cake for Ma's hen party tonight." Alvin shuffled his feet shyly, his cheeks reddening.

Melody sighed. She was grateful for his business, but suspected he purposely cut his order in two so he had an excuse to drop by twice today. She would have preferred efficiency, but good manners and a genuine fondness for the sheriff prevented her from showing any exasperation. She should be flattered by his attention—she knew, but she really wasn't interested in a romantic relationship at this point in her life. Not that he wasn't handsome, in his own way, but he was just not her type, she supposed, even if she *were* in the market for a romantic relationship. She took a quick moment to evaluate his appearance. He possessed the long, lean lines of a thoroughbred, but somehow wasn't able to project his inherent attractiveness, even in uniform. Perhaps it was his constant grinning. It made him appear a little strange, no, that wasn't really it; it was more his inability to realize his own appeal, a slight insecurity, an awkwardness. She mentally shook herself and focused on the business at hand.

"Not a problem, Al. Always good to see you!" she said, forcing a smile.

She felt a pang of guilt at her fib, but knew she probably made his day with her comment. In spite of her uncanny ability to notice and discern the overt as well as hidden attributes of others, Melody possessed a baffling blindness to her own qualities. She could have easily graced the pages of any girlie magazine, even in jeans and her trademark logoed tee. An Irish beauty, Melody was blessed with more than her fair share of pluses: glossy auburn, shoulder-length tresses (albeit piled on her head and anchored with a hairnet), an angelic face, and statuesque curves to rival any pin-up girl. She had many secret (and not so secret) male admirers in town, but even though she was consistently friendly and courteous, she possessed an intimidating blend of self-assurance, the formerly discussed unawareness of her beauty, and a steadfast personal rule against flirting.

"What kind of cake did you have in mind? We have a

cream cheese-filled red velvet and an orange-hickory nut on hand. Kerry made them yesterday, and they're still fresh."

As if summoned by her name, Kerry rushed in, flinging out hyper apologies as she whipped on an apron over her uniform of sparkly blue jeans and the shop's logo-emblazoned t-shirt.

"Where were you?" Melody asked.

"I forgot my phone in my car and wanted to make sure Aunt Rita didn't call with her family reunion order. I told her to call the shop rather than my cell, but she never remembers the number and can't be bothered to look it up. Good thing I checked; as she did leave me a voicemail with what she wants, and she's hoping to get everything tomorrow afternoon, even though the reunion doesn't start until Friday evening!" Kerry's words tumbled over each other as her hands gestured wildly. Melody wondered how Kerry was able to breathe while talking at such a rate.

"I see you've gone over your quota of caffeine today," Melody teased, noting Kerry's messy blond bun slipping out of the hair net stretched crookedly over her head and the slight sheen of sweat on her brow.

Kerry, plump and pretty, was engaged to Port Warren High's beloved football coach, George Stanley, who adored her. In Kerry's mind, this gave her free reign to play matchmaker with all her unfortunately single friends and acquaintances, especially her beautiful boss.

"Yeah, might have overdone the go-juice just a tad." Kerry chuckled, tucking her stray blond strands back into the net. Kerry then turned her attention to their visitor. "Hey, Al, you forget something? Weren't you in earlier?"

Alvin blushed and nodded, looking down at his shoes and rubbing his close-cropped brown hair.

Kerry smiled wickedly at his obvious discomfiture. "I'm beginning to think this is your new office!"

Melody gave her a quick, pursed-lip glare, knowing it would only encourage her would-be marriage broker to continue to tease poor Alvin.

"Yep, completely forgot about Ma's card deal tonight;

she wanted me to pick up a cake; whatcha got in stock?" Alvin asked trying to recover himself.

As the sheriff switched his embarrassed attention to his torturer, Melody took the opportunity to slip quietly back into the kitchen to finish the croissants, leaving Kerry to fill Alvin's order. She concentrated, cutting and folding thin strips into perfect crescents.

"That guy's got it bad!" Kerry announced as she sailed into the kitchen, automatically beelining it for the coffee machine.

"No! You're cut off!" Melody was quick to see her assistant's intention and she grabbed Kerry's sleeve with a floury hand, "No more coffee for you!"

Kerry sheepishly set the pot back down and crossed her arms. She eyed the tray of bakery rejects that failed Melody's perfectionistic eye, sighed, and helped herself to a broken cookie. Nibbling, she glared at Melody.

"You've got it bad," Melody insisted. "You're torturing that poor man, and you know it! What did he end up buying?"

"Don't try and change the subject! That dog is one

whipped puppy. If he really forgot that cake this morning, I'm a one-eyed frog. His mom has bridge every Wednesday night, tonight is no exception!" Kerry exclaimed while munching through a second cookie reject.

Melody shrugged, not wanting to encourage that line of thinking. She'd known for a while that Alvin had a thing for her. She tried her best to ignore it and avoid him as much as possible. With her busy schedule, she just wasn't ready for anything serious, even if it was with someone like Alvin. Or was it really about her schedule? Whatever, she was just not into a relationship at the moment. She had to admit, he was a good guy. And he would probably treat her right if she ever gave him a chance. But it was just too soon.

"He's either going to have to man up and ask you out or go broke buying donuts and cakes! For a lawman, he ain't very brave!" Kerry added.

Melody let her rattle on, hoping Kerry would run out of words on the subject, though that seemed unlikely.

Kerry propped her chin on her left palm looking all dreamy. "I think he's cute, though, don't you? A little on the puppy dog side, but still pretty manly when he's not tripping over his tongue when you're around."

Melody sighed, rolled her eyes, and kept silent. It was her weapon of choice and it worked well with Kerry, whose main hobby was verbalizing, combined with taking off on frequent, caffeine-infused rabbit trails. So, Kerry prattled on while Mel took a moment to mull over the situation.

In truth, she almost wished she reciprocated Alvin's apparent feelings. She dreaded the day she would really have to reject such a nice guy. She blew out a breath of frustration, hoping against hope that he would never find the courage to approach her romantically because in that way she could avoid the whole ordeal. If he did ever find the courage to ask her out, she would just have to find a nice way to turn him down. Maybe she should start thinking about how she could get out of it without hurting his feelings.

Her thoughts, generally practical, quickly switched over to Aunt Rita's reunion and she broke into Kerry's monologue.

"Which cake did the sheriff end up buying? And what does Aunt Rita need by Friday?" Melody asked and Kerry cooperated with the subject change, her talking talent showcased by her ability to jump off and on any topic train.

"He decided on the red velvet. Auntie said she needs three cakes: one devil's food, one pineapple upside down, and one hummingbird. I think I should call her and steer her away from the hummingbird, as it's too similar to the pineapple upside-down—don't you think? Maybe a pecan Texas sheet instead? Add a little variety? Also, she wants two-dozen each of chocolate chip, shortbread and peanut butter cookies, an apple strudel and six dozen dinner rolls. I think I better tell her to freeze everything when she gets it tomorrow since she's not serving most of it until Saturday and Sunday, and I wouldn't think she'd like them anything but fresh. Really, she should get everything from us Friday afternoon; we could have it done by two, don't you think? Maybe I should call her? Maybe not, as she never changes her mind once she makes a plan; maybe you should call her? She'd probably listen to you better than me. But maybe freezing them would be good enough and then we wouldn't be as stressed on Saturday, as we have that wedding cake to deliver and set up, and Jeannette isn't somebody we want to disappoint with shoddy work..." Kerry continued to ponder the quandary of her aunt's order while she bustled about wiping counters, putting away clean tools from the dish drainer, and checking—and double-checking—the stores of supplies.

Just then the bell dinged, heralding another customer, and Kerry whisked out of the kitchen.

Melody opened the oven and placed the croissant trays inside, setting the timer as she finished. She could hear Kerry's voice, presumably talking to a customer, and while tempted to start on tomorrow's orders, she knew she should make an appearance in the shop as some of her customers took it very personally when she was too busy to greet them.

Kerry's Aunt Rita stood at the counter, her lips pursed as she listened to her niece's flood of advice. Rita held up her hand, finally getting Kerry to slow her word flow. Aunt Rita had a closet full of old-fashioned, 50's style dresses that belted at the waist, everything from floral, to stripes and plaids, to plain. She only ever wore dark brown, laced up walking shoes, white gloves, and netted hats whenever she ventured outside her house. Inside, she wore button-up housedresses, ones she deemed suitable for the constant cleaning she inflicted on her house. Dust was terrified to land anywhere in her vicinity.

"I need everything by tomorrow afternoon, Kerry Ann, is that going to be a problem?" Just as Kerry opened her mouth to answer, Rita caught sight of Melody.

"Thank God you're here! My niece seems to think I don't know my own mind, and I need her to understand that I need everything tomorrow afternoon. I will be extremely busy with other reunion tasks... of course, I have to do everything myself, the rest of the family cannot be trusted... so I need the desserts squared away tomorrow. Is that too difficult?" Rita glared at Melody belligerently.

"Oh no, Rita, tomorrow afternoon is perfect! We don't have another big order besides yours due until Friday afternoon, so it will work out just fine, and your choices show nice forethought and variety," Melody assured her.

"Hmph. Kerry Ann here seems to think I don't have enough variety in the cake department. I keep trying to explain that Cousin Harold loves the pineapple upside down and my sister must have hummingbird. There is no room for substitutes. Now, I need to know if those choices are going to be a problem? I don't want to take my business elsewhere, but my friend Alice's cousin bakes and sells cakes out of her kitchen, so I do have other options," Rita continued to scowl pugnaciously at her niece while she directed her question to Melody.

"No, we can certainly bake all your choices," Melody replied calmly. "All your selections are just fine, and there is no finer cake baker than your niece here!"

Mollified, Kerry let go of her need to adjust Aunt Rita's cake menu, and smiled at her employer, "Awww shucks, boss-lady! You're the best!"

"Hmph," Rita grunted, clutching her giant purse more firmly to her chest, as if perhaps Melody and Kerry weren't to be trusted; she then adjusted her old-fashioned hat and exited with, "Okay then. I'll expect your delivery tomorrow afternoon, but no earlier than two pm, as I'll need an afternoon rest with all this working myself to death. And for what? Some ungrateful relatives who don't mind reaping the benefits of all my back-breaking labor!"

Kerry groaned, shaking her head. As soon as her aunt was out of earshot, she commented, "Oh my God, Aunt Rita is something else, isn't she? No wonder Uncle Leroy left this earth... her sunny disposition probably poisoned him to death!"

Melody smiled, suspecting Kerry probably inherited her aunt's opinionated personality, and ability to talk at lightspeed. Though Kerry was liberally tempered with cheerfulness, Rita lacked

Grab the first 6 books in the Bakers and Bulldogs series in this box set for FREE with Kindle Unlimited here

This little bundle of Frenchie love would appreciate it too, this is Lila, also known as Piggy Pig.

Printed in Great Britain
by Amazon